ILLUMINATION PRESENTS

minions
THE RISE OF GRU

Adapted by **DAVID LEWMAN**

Illustrated by **ALAN BATSON**

❦ A GOLDEN BOOK • NEW YORK

Minions 2: The Rise of Gru © 2022 Universal City Studios LLC. All Rights Reserved.
Published in the United States by Golden Books, an imprint of Random House Children's Books,
a division of Penguin Random House LLC, 1745 Broadway, New York, NY 10019, and in Canada by
Penguin Random House Canada Limited, Toronto. Golden Books, A Golden Book, A Little Golden Book,
the G colophon, and the distinctive gold spine are registered trademarks of Penguin Random House LLC.
rhcbooks.com
Educators and librarians, for a variety of teaching tools, visit us at RHTeachersLibrarians.com
ISBN 978-0-593-17303-9 (trade) — ISBN 978-0-593-17304-6 (ebook)
Printed in the United States of America
10 9 8 7 6 5 4 3

Years ago, a team of supervillains known as the **VICIOUS 6** wanted the powerful, ancient **ZODIAC STONE**. Their oldest member, **WILD KNUCKLES**, snuck into a creepy jungle temple to steal it.

But when Wild Knuckles returned with the Stone, **BELLE BOTTOM** and the other villains stole it from *him*! Wild Knuckles vowed to get the Stone back.

In another part of the world, a boy named **GRU** had recently started sixth grade. When his teacher asked what he wanted to be when he grew up, he answered, **"A supervillain!"**

All the other kids laughed at him.

But when he got home, Gru found
an invitation from the Vicious 6! He ran to his
new lair and told his **MINIONS**, "The Vicious 6 got
my application! They want to interview me tomorrow!"

The Minions cheered.

MINI BOSS!

MINI BOSS!

The next day, Gru went to a record store that had a secret entrance to the lair of the Vicious 6. He met **DR. NEFARIO**, a brilliantly evil scientist posing as the record store clerk. Dr. Nefario gave Gru his latest invention, the **STICKY HAND**.

"If you ever get famous," Dr. Nefario said, **"remember who gave you your first gadget!"**

Down in their headquarters, the Vicious 6 were surprised to find out Gru was just a kid! They rejected him, saying he was too young to join.

Their leader, Belle Bottom, laughed and said, **"Come back when you've done something to impress me!"**

Gru decided he would show them.
He used the Sticky Hand to steal the
Zodiac Stone!
"I'll get him!"
STRONGHOLD yelled.

Secretly spying on the Vicious 6, Wild Knuckles
saw Gru and the Minions with the Stone.

"Take the Stone back to the lair!"
Gru told **OTTO**, one of his Minions.

Gru was very excited when he returned to his lair. He figured he'd give the Stone back to the Vicious 6, and they'd be so impressed, they'd invite him to join their team of supervillains!

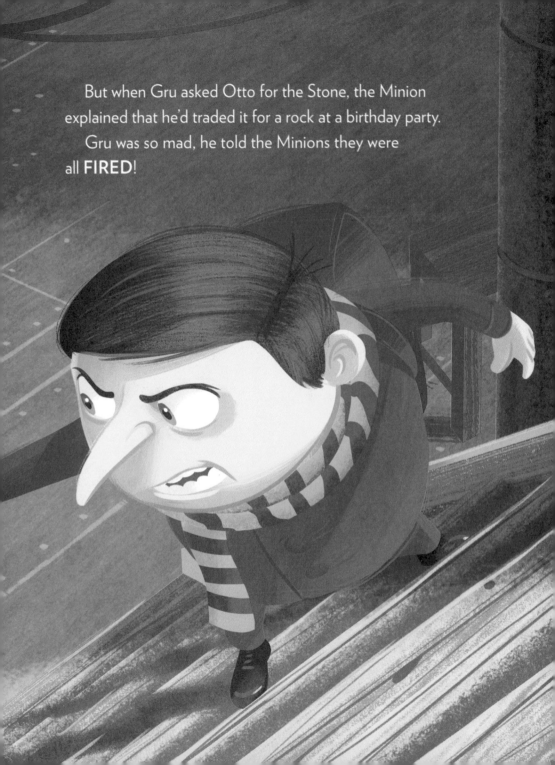

But when Gru asked Otto for the Stone, the Minion explained that he'd traded it for a rock at a birthday party. Gru was so mad, he told the Minions they were all **FIRED**!

Just as Gru set out to get the Stone back, he was taken by an orange van. It was Wild Knuckles and his henchmen! Gru was thrilled to hear how impressed Wild Knuckles was that he'd stolen something from the Vicious 6.

When Wild Knuckles discovered that Gru didn't have the Stone, he called **KEVIN** and told him he would trade their boss for the Stone.

Kevin, Stuart, and Bob went into the birthday party house to get the Stone back. The birthday boy explained that he had given it to his uncle. Meanwhile, outside of the party house, Otto saw the uncle ride off on a motorcycle and chased after him!

The other Minions decided they needed to get to San Francisco to save Gru, who was being held at Wild Knuckles' new lair, **DISCO INFERNO**.

At the airport, Kevin and Stuart disguised themselves as pilots. Bob dressed as a flight attendant.

The ride was a **little bumpy** but they managed to fly a plane to San Francisco!

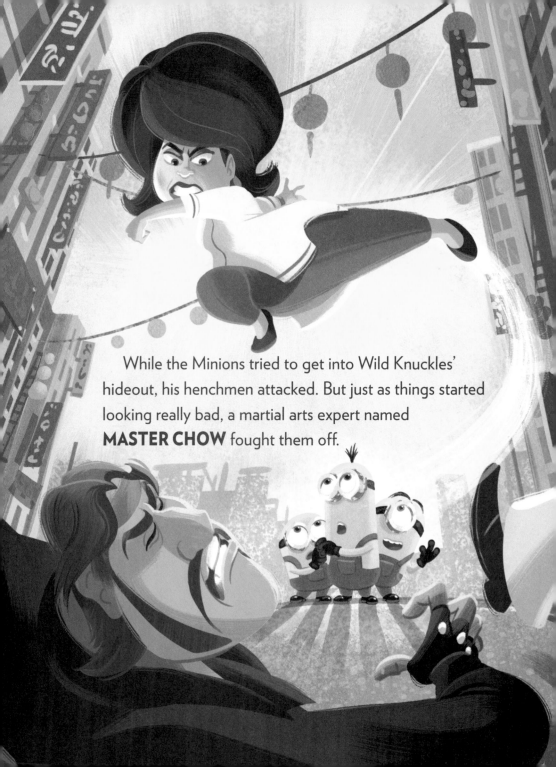

While the Minions tried to get into Wild Knuckles' hideout, his henchmen attacked. But just as things started looking really bad, a martial arts expert named **MASTER CHOW** fought them off.

The Minions asked Master Chow for kung fu lessons.
She firmly said NO . . . until Bob used his puppy-dog eyes . . .
and then so did Kevin and Stuart.

On their search for Gru and the Stone, the Vicious 6
learned that Gru was with Wild Knuckles at his lair.
By this time, Otto had gotten the Stone back!

Master Chow tried to teach kung fu to the Minions. They weren't exactly the best students, but they kept trying. Eventually, Master Chow declared them ready and sent them on their way.

YEAHH!

Back at Disco Inferno, Gru had been untied to help out around the house. Suddenly, Wild Knuckles fell into his own crocodile pool!

Instead of taking the chance to escape, Gru decided to help Wild Knuckles out. He couldn't leave his favorite villain like this!

Wild Knuckles offered to teach Gru some things since the young villain had saved his life. Working together, they successfully pulled off a heist at the Bank of Evil!

Unable to find Wild Knuckles or the Stone, the Vicious 6 destroyed Wild Knuckles' lair while the Minions watched from outside.

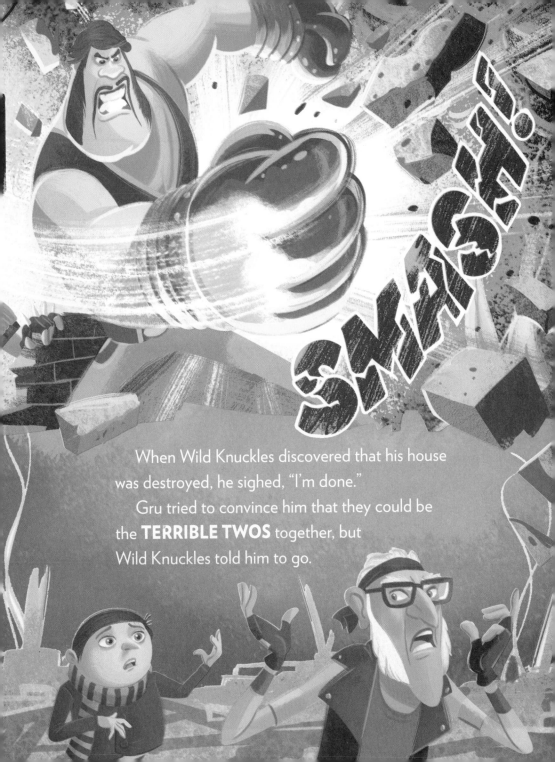

SMASH!

When Wild Knuckles discovered that his house was destroyed, he sighed, "I'm done."

Gru tried to convince him that they could be the **TERRIBLE TWOS** together, but Wild Knuckles told him to go.

Gru took the trolley to Chinatown—and there he found Otto! The Minion gave Gru the Stone. The young villain was confident that he could set things right and come out on top as a

MASTER SUPERVILLAIN!